Frankenstein

MARY SHELLEY

Adapted by Bob Blaisdell
Illustrated by Thea Kliros

DOVER PUBLICATIONS, INC.
Mineola, New York

DOVER CHILDREN'S THRIFT CLASSICS
EDITOR OF THIS VOLUME: SUSAN L. RATTINER

Copyright

Published in Canada by General Publishing Company, Ltd., 30 Lesmill Road, Don Mills, Toronto, Ontario.

Published in the United Kingdom by Constable and Company, Ltd., 3 The Lanchesters, 162–164 Fulham Palace Road, London W6 9ER.

Bibliographical Note

This Dover edition, first published in 1997, is a new abridgment of a standard edition. The illustrations have been prepared specially for the present edition.

Library of Congress Cataloging-in-Publication Data

Shelley, Mary Wollstonecraft, 1797–1851.
    Frankenstein / Mary Shelley ; adapted by Bob Blaisdell ; illustrated by Thea Kliros.
       p.   cm. — (Dover children's thrift classics)
    "This Dover edition . . . is a new abridgment of a standard edition. The illustrations have been prepared specially for the present edition"—Bib. note.
    Summary: A monster assembled by a scientist from parts of dead bodies develops a mind of his own as he learns to loathe himself and hate his creator.
    ISBN 0-486-29930-9 (pbk.)
    [1. Monsters—Fiction. 2. Horror stories.] I. Blaisdell, Robert. II. Kliros, Thea, ill. III. Title. IV. Series.
PZ7.S54145Fu   1997
[Fic]—dc21
                                                  97-11617
                                                    CIP
                                                      AC

Manufactured in the United States of America
Dover Publications, Inc., 31 East 2nd Street, Mineola, N.Y. 11501

Contents

As I walk in the streets of Petersburg, I feel a cold northern breeze.

1. The Arctic Ocean Stranger

St. Petersburg, Russia, December 11, 17—
My dear sister Margaret,

I address this journal to you, in England, in the hope that one day you will receive it.

I am already far north of London; and as I walk in the streets of Petersburg, I feel a cold northern breeze, which has traveled from the regions toward which I am destined to go. I cannot believe that the North Pole is the home of frost and emptiness; it presents itself to my imagination as the region of beauty and delight. There, Margaret, the sun is forever visible. There snow and frost have disappeared; and, sailing over a calm sea, we may sail to a land more wonderful and beautiful than any ever seen. What may not be expected in a country of eternal light? I may there discover the power of magnetism, which attracts the needle of a compass. I shall satisfy my curiosity with the sight of a part of the world never before visited. Think of the benefit I shall bestow on all mankind by discovering near the pole a passage to those other countries.

My courage is strong; but my hopes waver, and I am often depressed. I am about to proceed on a long and difficult voyage, one that will demand all my strength. I must not only keep up the spirits of my sailors, but also sometimes my own, when theirs are failing.

Archangel, Russia, March 28, 17—

I have hired a vessel and am busy collecting my sailors. But there is one thing I lack. I have no friend, Margaret, with whom to share my joy. I am twenty-eight and as uneducated as many schoolboys. I greatly need a friend who would try to improve my mind.

Well, these are useless complaints; I shall certainly find no friend on the wide ocean, nor even here in Archangel, on the White Sea, among merchants and seamen.

It is impossible to describe for you the trembling, half pleasurable and half fearful, with which I am preparing to set out. I am going to unexplored regions of the Arctic Ocean, to "the land of mist and snow."

July 7, 17—

I am well advanced on my voyage. I am in good spirits; my men are bold and determined, and the floating sheets of ice that pass us do not appear to bother them. We have already reached a very high latitude; but it is the height of summer, and although it is not so warm as in England, the southern gales, which blow us toward those shores I wish to reach, give us a surprising warmth.

August 5, 17—

So strange an accident has happened that I have to write it all down, although it is very likely that you will see me before these journals can be sent to you.

Last Monday (July 31) we were nearly surrounded by ice, which closed in the ship on all sides. Our situation was somewhat dangerous, especially as we were enveloped by a very thick fog. We held fast, hoping that some change would take place.

About two o'clock the mist cleared away, and we beheld, stretched out in every direction, vast plains of ice, which seemed to have no end. Some of my comrades groaned, and I began to grow anxious, when a strange sight suddenly attracted our attention. We saw

A being in the shape of a man sat in the sledge and guided the dogs.

a low carriage, fixed on a sledge and drawn by dogs, pass on toward the north, at the distance of half a mile; a being that had the shape of a man, but apparently of gigantic stature, sat in the sledge and guided the dogs. We watched the rapid progress of the traveler with our telescopes until he disappeared.

This vision excited our wonder. We were, we believed, many hundred miles from any land; but this sighting of a man seemed to suggest that it was not so distant as we had supposed. Shut in by the ice, however, we could not follow his track.

Before night the ice broke and freed a path for our ship. We, however, lay to until the morning, fearing to meet in the dark those large loose masses that float about after the breaking up of the ice. I made use of this time to rest for a few hours.

In the morning, however, as soon as it was light, I went upon the deck and found all the sailors busy on one side of the vessel, apparently talking to someone in the sea. It was, in fact, a sledge, like the one we' had seen before, which had drifted toward us in the night on a large piece of ice. Only one dog remained alive; but there was a human being within it whom the sailors were trying to talk into coming aboard. He was not, as the other traveler seemed to be, a native of some undiscovered island, but a European. When I appeared on deck, the shipmaster said, "Here is our captain, and he will not allow you to perish on the open sea."

On seeing me, the stranger addressed me in English, although with a foreign accent. "Before I come on board your vessel," said he, "will you have the kindness to inform me where you are going?"

You may guess my surprise on hearing such a question addressed to me from a man on the brink of death and to whom I supposed my vessel would have been salvation. I replied, however, that we were on a voyage of discovery toward the North Pole.

Upon hearing this, he appeared satisfied and agreed to come on board. Good God! Margaret, if you had seen the man who bargained in this way, your surprise would have been boundless. His arms and legs were nearly frozen, his body thin and worn out. I never saw a man in so wretched a condition. We tried to carry him into the cabin, but as soon as he left the fresh air, he fainted. We brought him back to the deck and restored him by rubbing him with brandy and forcing him to drink a small dose. As soon as he showed signs of life, we wrapped him up in blankets and placed him near the chimney of the kitchen stove. Slowly he recovered and ate a little soup.

Two days passed in this way before he was able to speak, and I often feared that his sufferings had stolen his wits. When he had in some degree recovered, I had him moved to my own cabin and attended to him as much as my duty would permit. I never saw a more interesting creature: his eyes have generally a wild expression, but there are moments when, if anyone performs an act of kindness toward him, his whole face lights up with goodness and sweetness. But he is generally sad, and sometimes he gnashes his teeth.

When my guest was a little recovered, I had great trouble keeping the men from asking him a thousand questions. The lieutenant asked why he had come so far upon the ice in so strange a vehicle.

The sufferer's face became gloomy, and he replied, "To seek the one who fled from me."

"And did the man you are chasing travel in the same way?"

"Yes."

"Then I fancy we have seen him, for the day before we picked you up, we saw some dogs drawing a sledge with a man in it, across the ice."

This aroused the stranger's attention, and he asked many questions concerning the route that the demon, as he called him, had taken. Soon after, when he was alone with me, he said, "I have, doubtless, excited your curiosity, as well as that of these good people; but you are too considerate to ask questions."

"Certainly. It would indeed be very rude of me to trouble you."

"And yet you rescued me from a strange and dangerous situation; you have kindly restored me to life."

Soon after this he asked if I thought that the breaking

up of the ice had destroyed the other sledge. I replied that the ice had not broken until nearly midnight, and the traveler might have arrived at a safe place before then.

From this moment the stranger wished to be up on deck as much as possible to watch for the sledge that we had seen; but I have persuaded him to remain in the cabin, for he is far too weak to bear the frigid air. I have promised him that someone will watch for him and give him immediate news if any such sledge should appear.

The stranger has gradually improved in health but is very silent and appears uneasy when anyone except me enters the cabin. Yet his manners are so gentle that the sailors are all interested in him. For my own part, I begin to love him as a brother, and his constant and deep grief fills me with sympathy. He must have been a fine man in his better days, being even now so attractive and good.

I said in one of my earlier entries, my dear Margaret, that I should find no friend on the wide ocean; yet I have found a man who, before his spirit had been broken by misery, I should have been happy to have had as a friend.

August 13, 17—

My guest is now much recovered from his illness and is continually on the deck, watching for the sledge. Although unhappy, he interests himself deeply in the projects of others. He has often talked with me on mine. I told him how gladly I would sacrifice my fortune, my life, my every hope, to the success of my quest. One man's life or death would be a small price to pay for the knowledge I looked for, to find a passage through the polar waters to the Pacific.

As I spoke of such willing sacrifice, a dark gloom spread over his face, and finally a groan burst from him. I paused; at length he spoke: "Unhappy man! Do you share my madness? Hear me; let me tell my tale, and you will give up such ideas."

He asked me the story of my earlier years. I spoke of my desire of finding a friend, and that a man could hardly be happy who did not enjoy such a blessing.

"I agree with you," replied the stranger. "I once had a friend, the most noble of human creatures, and am entitled, therefore, to speak of friendship. You have hope, and the world before you, and have no cause for despair. But I—I have lost everything and cannot begin life anew."

As he said this, his face expressed grief; he became silent and returned to his cabin.

August 19, 17—

The stranger said to me, "You may easily see, Captain Walton, that I have suffered terrible misfortunes. I had decided at one time that the memory of these evils should die with me, but you have changed my mind. You seek for knowledge and wisdom, as I once did; and I truly hope that the result of your wishes may not be a snake to bite you, as mine has been. I do not know that the telling of my story will be useful to you; yet I imagine that you may find a moral for your own situation. Prepare to hear of occurrences that are usually called unbelievable. I cannot doubt, however, that with your knowledge of all the details, my tale will show its truth."

I felt the greatest eagerness to hear the story and said, "Yes, I am curious. I hope as well that I may be able to help you once I know your troubles."

"I thank you," he replied, "for your sympathy, but

there is no help. I wait but for one event, and then I shall rest in peace. Nothing can change my fate; listen to my story, and you will see how unchangeable it is."

He then told me that his name was Victor Frankenstein and that he would begin his story the next day, when I should have some time.

I have decided that every night, when I am not busy with my duties, I shall write down, as nearly as possible in his own words, what he has told me during the day. Even now, as I begin my task, his full-toned voice swells in my ears; his bright eyes fix on me with all their sad sweetness; I see his thin hand moving as he talks, while the lines on his face are lit up by his soul. Strange and frightening must be his story, terrible the storm that overtook such a fine vessel on its course and wrecked it!

2. Victor Frankenstein Begins His Story

I AM SWISS by birth, from Geneva, and my family is one of the most distinguished of that country. My father was respected by all who knew him for his honesty and civic-mindedness. He passed his younger days busy with the country's affairs, which prevented his marrying early. It was not until the end of his life that he became a husband and father.

There was a large difference between the ages of my parents, but this only seemed to bring them closer. He admired and respected her virtues. He did everything to fulfill her wishes and make life easy. Caroline had suffered as a girl, tending her weak and ill father, who had been my father's best friend. He tried to shelter her, as an exotic plant is sheltered by the gardener, and to surround her with all that could please her. Her health had been shaken by what she had gone through with her father. In the two years before their marriage, my father had gradually given up all his public duties; and immediately after their wedding they traveled to Italy, where she could rebuild her strength.

From Italy they visited Germany and France. I, their eldest child, was born in Naples, Italy, and as a young child went with them on their rambles. I remained for several years their only child. Much as they were attached to each other, they gave me unbounded love.

I was their plaything and idol—their child, the innocent and helpless creature given them by heaven.

For a long time I was their only care. When I was about five years old, they passed a week on the shores of Lake Como. Their kindness often made them visit the cottages of the poor. This, to my mother, was more than a duty; it was a passion.

During one of their walks, they discovered an unusually poor cottage, with a number of half-clothed children about it. One day, when my father had gone by himself to Milan, my mother and I visited this home. There was a hardworking peasant and his wife, bent down by care and labor, feeding a skimpy meal to five hungry children. Among these there was one who attracted my mother far above all the rest. The four others were dark-eyed, hardy little urchins; this child was thin and very fair. Her hair was gold, and her eyes blue and clear.

The peasant woman, seeing that my mother had fixed eyes of wonder and admiration on this lovely girl, told her story. She was not her child, but the daughter of a Milanese nobleman. Her mother, a German, had died giving birth to her. The infant had been placed with these good people to nurse: they were better off then. They had not been long married, and their eldest child was but just born. The child's father was shortly thereafter jailed or killed; no one ever knew. In either case his property and wealth were taken over by the government; his child became an orphan. She stayed with her foster parents and bloomed in their poor home.

When my father returned from Milan, he found playing with me in the hall of our villa a child fairer than a painted angel. My mother had asked her guardians to give her up to be raised by our family. They were fond of the sweet orphan, but it would be unfair, they

I looked upon Elizabeth as mine to protect, love, and cherish.

thought, to keep her in poverty when fortune offered her such a home. The result was that Elizabeth Lavenza became a child of my parents—my more than sister—the beautiful and adored companion of all my interests and pleasures.

Everyone loved Elizabeth. On the evening before she was brought to my home, my mother had said playfully, "I have a pretty present for Victor—tomorrow he shall have it."

And when, the next day, she presented Elizabeth to me as her promised gift, I looked upon Elizabeth as mine—mine to protect, love, and cherish. We called each other "cousin." No word, no expression could describe what she meant to me—my more than sister, since till death she was to be mine only.

We were brought up together; there was not quite a year's difference in our ages. While she admired the magnificent appearance of the world around our beautiful Swiss home, I delighted in looking for its origins and causes. The world was to me a secret that I desired to uncover. Curiosity about the hidden laws of nature is among the earliest feelings I remember.

On the birth of a second son, Ernest, my junior by seven years, my parents gave up their wandering life entirely and fixed themselves in their native country. We had a house in Geneva and country home in Belrive, the eastern shore of Como. We lived mostly in the country. Several years later another son, William, was born.

I cared little, in general, for my schoolmates. But I enjoyed the closest friendship with one—Henry Clerval, the son of a merchant in Geneva. He was talented and imaginative.

No human being could have passed a happier childhood than I. My parents were possessed by the spirit of kindness. They were the creators of all the many delights we enjoyed. When I mingled with other families, I noticed how fortunate I was, and I was grateful.

I was hot-tempered, however, and passionate. My passions led me not toward childish games but to an eager desire to learn. Yet I was not interested in the grammar of languages, the laws of governments, or politics. It was the secrets of heaven and earth that I desired to learn. Meanwhile Clerval busied himself with the stage of life; the virtues of heroes and the actions of men were his interest.

I feel pleasure in remembering my childhood, before bad luck colored my thoughts and changed them into gloominess. However, in telling the story of my early days, I also record those events that led to my misery, for when I would try to recall the moment of birth of that passion that later ruled my fate, I found it arose, like a river, from small and seemingly insignificant sources; but, swelling as it went on, it became the flood that has swept away all my hopes and joys.

3. Frankenstein's Monster

NATURAL SCIENCE IS the study that has led to my fate; I desire, therefore, in this story, to state those facts that led to my fondness for it. I have always had a longing to penetrate the secrets of nature. In spite of the hard work and wonderful discoveries of modern scientists, I always came away from my studies unsatisfied.

The uneducated peasant looked at the forces around him and knew their practical uses. The most learned scientist knew little more. He had partially uncovered the face of nature, but her deeper mysteries remained. He might take apart matter and give it names, but final causes were utterly unknown to him. I had tried to know nature, and I had given up.

But here were books and here were men who had penetrated deeper and knew more. I took them at their word, and I became their follower.

I was, to a great degree, self-taught with regard to my favorite studies. My father was not scientific, and I was left to struggle with a child's blindness trying to slake my thirst for knowledge. I entered into the search for the elixir of life. What glory would come to the discovery if I could keep disease from human beings and make man invulnerable to any but a violent death!

Nor were these my only visions. The raising of ghosts or devils was a promise given by my favorite authors;

and if my magic spells were always unsuccessful, I blamed myself rather than my instructors. And so for a time I was busy with impossible science, guided by my heated imagination and childish reasoning, till an accident again changed the current of my ideas.

When I was about fifteen years old, we had gone to our house near Belrive, where we witnessed a most violent and terrible thunderstorm. It came from behind the mountains of Jura, and the thunder burst with frightful loudness from various quarters of the heavens. I remained, while the storm lasted, watching its progress with curiosity and delight. As I stood at the door, I saw a stream of fire strike an old and beautiful oak that stood about twenty yards from our house; and as soon as the dazzling light vanished, the oak had dis-

I saw a stream of fire strike an old and beautiful oak tree near our house.

appeared, and nothing remained but an exploded stump.

Before this I did not know the laws of electricity. At this time a man of great research in natural science was visiting us, and he explained a theory he had formed on the subject of electricity and electric shock. All that had so long had my attention suddenly became worthless. I now made myself study mathematics and the other branches of science that had secure foundations.

When I reached the age of seventeen, my parents decided that I should become a student at the University of Ingolstadt. I had before attended the schools of Geneva, but my father thought it necessary for the completion of my education that I should be experienced in other customs and manners than those of my native country. But before the time I was to leave, the first misfortune of my life occurred—a sign of my future misery.

Elizabeth had caught the scarlet fever; her illness was severe, and she was in the greatest danger. During her illness we urged my mother not to be the nurse. She had first given in to us, but when she heard that the life of her favorite was in trouble, she could no longer hold herself back. She attended Elizabeth's sickbed; her nursing defeated the danger of the fever—Elizabeth was saved, but the results of this action were fatal to her rescuer. On the third day my mother sickened.

On her deathbed this best of women retained her personal strength and kindness. She joined the hands of Elizabeth and me.

"My children," she said, "my hopes of future happiness were on the prospect of your marriage. This expectation will now be the hope of your father. Elizabeth, my love, you must supply my place to my younger children. Alas! I regret that I am taken from you; and, happy and beloved as I have been, it is hard to leave you all. But these are not good thoughts; I will try to prepare myself cheerfully for death and will hope to meet you in another world."

She died calmly, and her face expressed affection even in death. I need not describe the feelings of those whose dearest relationships are cut off by death. It is so long before the mind can tell itself that she, whom we saw every day and whose very life appeared a part of our own, can have left forever. My mother was dead, but we had still duties to perform; we had to continue our course and learn to consider ourselves lucky for the loved ones whom death has not taken.

My leaving for Ingolstadt, which had been delayed by these events, was now again decided upon. The day of my departure arrived. Clerval spent the last evening with us. He had tried to persuade his father to allow him to accompany me and to become my fellow student, but in vain. His father was a narrow-minded trader and saw idleness and ruin in the educational ambitions of his son.

When at dawn I went down to the carriage that was to take me away, they were all there—my father to bless me, Clerval to shake my hand, my Elizabeth to tell me to write often to her.

I threw myself into the carriage and started away. I, who had ever been surrounded by kind friends, was now alone. My journey to Ingolstadt was long and tiring. At length the white steeple of the town met my eyes. I got out and was brought to my room to spend the evening as I pleased.

The next morning I delivered my letters of introduction and paid a visit to some of the professors. Chance led me first to Monsieur Krempe, professor of natural science. He was an unrefined and rude man, but deeply knowledgeable of the secrets of science. He asked me several questions concerning my progress in the different branches of science. I mentioned the names of the principal authors I had studied. The professor stared. "Have you," he said, "really spent your time in studying such nonsense?"

"Yes."

"My dear sir, you must begin your studies entirely anew."

So saying, he stepped aside and wrote down a list of several books of natural science that he wanted me to read, and dismissed me after mentioning that in the beginning of the following week he intended to begin a course of general lectures on natural science and that Monsieur Waldman, a fellow professor, would lecture on chemistry on alternate days.

Although I could not agree to go hear that little conceited fellow Krempe deliver lectures, I did attend Monsieur Waldman's. This professor was very unlike his colleague. He appeared about fifty years of age, with a kind face; a few gray hairs covered his temples, but those at the back of his head were nearly black. He was short but stood straight up; and his voice was the sweetest I had ever heard.

Monsieur Waldman began his lecture with a review of the history of chemistry and the various improvements made by different men of learning. He then took a quick view of the present state of the science and explained many of its elementary terms. After having made a few experiments, he concluded the day with a short speech, which I shall never forget:

The ancient teachers of this science [the very ones I had studied at home] promised impossibilities and performed nothing. The modern masters promise very little. They know that one metal cannot be changed into another and that the elixir of life is a fantasy. But these scientists, who seem only to dabble in dirt and to hunch over the microscope, have indeed performed miracles. They see into the depths of nature and show how she works in her hiding places. They go up into the heavens; they have discovered how the blood circulates, and the nature of the air we breathe. They have acquired new and almost unlimited powers; they can command the thunders of heaven, mimic the earthquake, and even mock the invisible world with its own shadows.

Such were the professor's words—rather, let me say, the words of fate—that came to destroy me. As he went on, my mind was filled with one thought, one idea, one purpose. So much has been done, exclaimed the soul of Frankenstein—more, far more, will I achieve; walking in their footsteps, I will pioneer a new way, explore unknown powers, and unfold to the world the deepest mysteries of creation.

The next day I paid Monsieur Waldman a visit. His manners in private were even more mild and attractive than in public. I gave him the same account of my former studies as I had given to Monsieur Krempe. He heard with attention the little story concerning my studies and smiled at the authors' names, but without mocking me. He said that "these were men to whose untiring work modern scientists were indebted for most of the foundations of their knowledge. Their work has made ours easier. The work of men of genius is nearly always a boon to mankind." I asked him to recommend some books.

"If your wish," said Monsieur Waldman, "is to become really a man of science and not merely a petty experimentalist, I should advise you to study every branch of natural science, including mathematics."

He then took me into his laboratory and explained to me the uses of his various machines, instructing me as

*He took me into his laboratory and showed me
how to use the machines.*

to what I ought to buy and promising me the use of his own when I should have advanced far enough in the science. He also gave me the list of books I had requested, and I left.

Thus ended a memorable day for me; it decided my destiny.

From this day natural science, especially chemistry, became nearly my sole occupation. I read those works on these subjects. I attended the lectures and became acquainted with the scientists of the university, and I found even in Monsieur Krempe a great deal of sound sense and information, combined, it is true, with rudeness. In Monsieur Waldman I found a true friend.

Because I studied so hard, my progress was rapid. Two years passed in my studies, during which time I paid no visit to Geneva. In other studies you go as far as others have gone before you, and there is nothing more to know; but in a scientific study there is always food for discovery and wonder. At the end of two years, I made some discoveries in the improvement of some chemical instruments, which gained me great admiration at the university. At this point, because my professors had no more to teach me, I thought of returning to my friends and my native town, but something happened that kept me there.

One of the studies that had especially attracted me was the structure of the human frame. Where, I often asked myself, did the principle of life originate? It was a bold question, the answer to which has always been shrouded in mystery. I determined from then on to apply myself to those branches of science that relate to physiology, the study of the body. Had I not had tremendous enthusiasm, this study would have been dull and almost intolerable. To examine the causes of life, we must first have the examination of death. I studied anatomy, but this was not enough; I must also observe the natural decay of the human body.

I had no supernatural horrors. To me a graveyard was merely the place that received dead bodies. Now I was led to look at the cause and progress of this decay and forced to spend days and nights in tombs. I saw how the fine form of man broke down and wasted away; I saw the worms take over our soft tissues. I paused, examining and analyzing all the details that showed the change from life to death and death to life, until from the midst of this darkness a sudden light broke in upon me—a light so brilliant and wondrous, yet so simple, that while I became dizzy with what it revealed, I was surprised that after so many men of genius who had tried to do so, I alone discovered so astonishing a secret.

Remember, I am not recording the vision of a madman. The stages of discovery were distinct and probable. After days and nights of incredible labor, I succeeded in discovering the cause of life; even more, I became myself capable of bringing to life lifeless matter. What had been the study and desire of the wisest men since the creation of the world was now within my grasp.

I see by your eagerness and the wonder and hope that your eyes express, my friend, that you expect to be informed of the secret that I know; that cannot be. Listen patiently until the end of my story, and you will understand why I will not talk about it. Learn from me, at least by example, how dangerous is knowledge and how much happier is that man who believes his native town to be the world than he who tries to become greater than his nature will allow.

When I found so astonishing a power placed within my hands, I hesitated a long time concerning the manner in which I should use it. Although I had the power to animate matter, yet to prepare a body, with all its fibers, muscles, and veins, still remained a work of unimaginable difficulty. I doubted at first whether I should try to create a being like myself or one of simpler organization; but my imagination was too excited by my first success to doubt my ability to give life to an animal as complex as man.

I prepared myself for many failures, but I never doubted that I would finally succeed. As the smallness of the parts slowed down my work, I decided to make a being of gigantic stature; that is to say, about eight feet in height. After having spent some months in collecting and arranging my materials, I began.

A new species would bless me as its creator. Many happy and excellent creatures would owe their existence to me. No father could claim the gratitude of his child so completely as I would deserve theirs. I thought that if I could animate lifeless matter, I might in time (although I now found it impossible) renew life where death had come.

During the night, I collected bones, organs, and flesh from tombs.

The moon gazed on my midnight labors while I chased nature to her hiding places. I collected bones, organs, and flesh from tombs. In a cell at the top of the house, separated from all the other apartments by a staircase, I kept my workshop of creation. The dissecting room and the slaughterhouse gave me many of my materials; and often I turned with loathing and disgust from what I was doing even as I brought my work near to completion.

The summer months passed while I was so engaged, heart and soul, in one project. My father did not scold me in his letters and took notice of my silence only by asking what I was studying. Every night I had a fever, and I became nervous; the fall of a leaf startled me, and I shunned my fellow creatures as if I had been guilty of a crime.

It was a dreary night in November when I beheld the fulfillment of my work. I collected the instruments of life around me, hoping that I might infuse a spark of being into the lifeless thing that lay at my feet. It was already one in the morning; the rain pattered against the panes, and my candle was nearly burned out when, by the glimmer of the light, I saw the dull yellow eye of the creature open; it breathed hard, and a convulsion jolted its arms and legs.

How can I describe my emotions or the wretch whom I had created? His limbs were in proportion to his body, and I had selected his features as beautiful. Great God! His yellow skin scarcely covered the work of muscles and arteries beneath; his hair was lustrous black and flowing, his teeth pearly white; but these features only formed a more horrid contrast with his watery eyes, shriveled complexion, and straight black lips.

For nearly two years I had worked hard, with the sole purpose of giving life to a lifeless body. For this I had deprived myself of rest and health. Now that I had finished, the beauty of the dream vanished, and breathless horror and disgust filled my heart. Unable to bear the sight of the being I had created, I rushed out of the room and continued a long time walking back and forth across my bedroom, unable to sleep. At last I threw myself on the bed in my clothes and slept, but I was disturbed by the wildest dreams. I started from my sleep with horror.

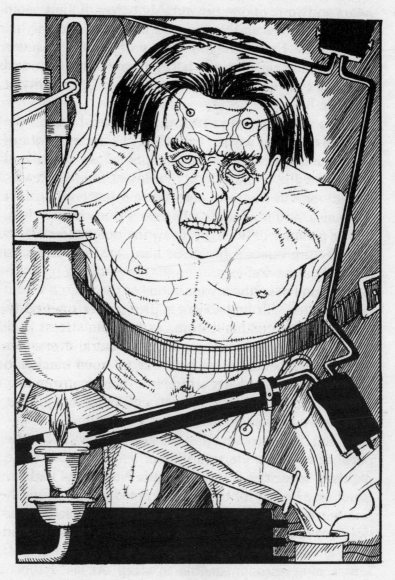

I beheld the wretch—the miserable monster I had created.

By the dim and yellow light of the moon, as it forced its way through the window shutters, I beheld the wretch—the miserable monster I had created. He held up the curtain of the bed; and his eyes were fixed on me. His jaws opened, and he muttered some sounds as a grin wrinkled his cheeks. He might have spoken, but I did not hear; one hand was stretched out, seemingly to stop me, but I escaped and rushed downstairs.

I hid in the courtyard belonging to the house where I lived, and I remained there the rest of the night, walking up and down, listening, fearing each sound as if it were announcing the approach of the demonical corpse to which I had so miserably given life.

Oh! No man could stand the horror of that face. I had gazed on him while unfinished; he was ugly then, but when those muscles and joints were able to move, he became unimaginably uglier.

At length morning dawned. The porter opened the gates of the court, and I ran out into the streets. I did not dare to return to my apartment, but at every turning I feared meeting the wretch. I continued walking for some time, trying, by exercise, to ease my mind. I crossed the streets without any clear idea of where I was or what I was doing.

I soon came to the inn at which the various coaches and carriages usually stopped. For some reason I paused here; but I remained some minutes with my eyes on a coach that was coming toward me from the other end of the street. As it drew nearer, I saw that it was a Swiss vehicle; it stopped just where I was standing, and as the door opened, I saw Henry Clerval, who, on seeing me, instantly sprang out. "My dear Frankenstein," exclaimed he, "how glad I am to see you! How lucky that you should be here at the very moment of my arrival!"

Nothing could equal my delight in seeing him; I grasped his hand and in a moment forgot my horror and misfortune; I felt suddenly, and for the first time during many months, calm and joyful. I welcomed my friend, and we walked toward my college.

Clerval said, "You may imagine how great the difficulty was to persuade my father that all necessary knowledge is not contained in bookkeeping. But his affection for me eventually overcame his dislike of education, and he has permitted me to come here to college."

"It gives me great delight to see you; but tell me how are my father, brothers, and Elizabeth."

"Very well and very happy, only a little worried that they hear from you so seldom. But my dear Frankenstein," he said, gazing directly into my weary eyes, "I did not before notice how very ill you appear; so thin and pale; you look as if you had not slept for several nights."

"You have guessed right; I have lately been so deeply buried in one project that I have not allowed myself enough rest, as you see; but I hope that this project is now at an end and that I am finally free."

I could not bear to think of the event of the past night. I walked quickly, and we soon arrived at my college. I then reflected that the creature I had left in my apartment might still be there, alive and walking about. I dreaded seeing this monster, but I feared still more that Henry might see him. Asking him, then, to remain a few minutes at the bottom of the stairs, I darted up toward my room. I threw the door open, as children do when they expect a ghost to stand waiting for them on the other side; but nothing appeared. I stepped in: the apartment was empty. I could hardly believe that so great a good fortune could have come to me, but when

I saw that my enemy had fled, I clapped my hands for joy and ran down to Clerval.

He at first attributed my high spirits to his arrival, but when he watched me more carefully, he saw a wildness in my eyes, and my loud, strange laughter frightened him.

"My dear Victor," he cried, "what is the matter? Do not laugh that way. How ill you are! What is the cause of all this?"

"Do not ask me," I cried, putting my hands before my eyes, for I imagined I saw the dreaded creature glide into the room. "Oh, save me! Save me!" I fell down in a fit.

4. Illness and Death

THIS WAS THE beginning of a nervous fever that confined me for several months. During all that time Henry was my only nurse. He spared my father and Elizabeth the news of the severity of my illness. Surely nothing but his unbounded attention could have restored me to life.

Slowly, but with frequent relapses, I recovered. In a short time I became as cheerful as I had been before I developed my passion for creating life.

"Dearest Clerval," I exclaimed, "how kind, how very good you are to me. This whole winter, instead of pursuing your studies, as you promised yourself, you have attended me in my sick room. How shall I ever repay you?"

"I may speak to you on one subject, may I not?"

I trembled. One subject! What could it be? Could he talk about something about which I dared not even speak?

"Calm yourself," said Clerval, "I will not mention it if it bothers you; but your father and cousin would be very happy if they received a letter from you in your own handwriting. They hardly know how ill you have been and are worried at the long silence."

"Is that all, my dear Henry? Of course my first thought is of those dear, dear friends I love!"

"If this is so, my friend, you will perhaps be glad to

see a letter that has been lying here some days for you; it is from your cousin, I believe."

Clerval then put the following letter into my hands. It was from my own Elizabeth:

My dearest cousin,

You have been ill, and even the constant letters from dear kind Henry are not enough to reassure me on your account. You are forbidden to write—to hold a pen; yet one word from you, dear Victor, is necessary to calm our fears.

Get well—and return to us. You will find a happy, cheerful home and friends who love you dearly. Your father's health is good, and he asks but to see you. How pleased you would be to see your younger brother Ernest. He is now sixteen and full of energy and spirit. He looks upon studying as hateful; he spends his time in the open air, climbing the hills or rowing on the lake. I fear that he will become an idler unless we allow him to do as he wishes and enter a military career in a distant country.

Little change, except the growth of the dear children, has taken place since you left us. I must say a few words to you, my dear cousin, of little darling William. I wish you could see him; he is very tall for his age, with sweet blue eyes, dark eyelashes, and curling hair. When he smiles, two little dimples appear on each cheek.

I have written myself into a better mood, dear cousin; but my worry about you returns upon me as I finish. Write, dearest Victor—one line, one word will be a blessing to us. Ten thousand thanks to Henry for his kindness and his letters. Adieu! My cousin, take care of yourself, and, I beg you, write!

Elizabeth
Geneva, March 18, 17—

"Dear, dear Elizabeth!" I said when I had read her letter. "I will write instantly and relieve them from worrying." I wrote, and this action greatly tired me; but my health was returning, and in another two weeks I was able to leave my chamber.

Clerval had come to the university to make himself the complete master of Oriental languages, and he easily persuaded me, fed up with science, to study with him. I felt great relief in being the fellow pupil with my friend, and found not only instruction but peace in the works of the Orientalists. When you read their writings, life appears to consist of a warm sun and a garden of roses.

Clerval had come to the university, and I studied with him.

Summer passed away in these studies, and my return to Geneva was fixed for the end of fall; but I was delayed by several events, and winter and snow arrived, making the roads impassable. I put off my journey until the spring.

The month of May had already come, and every day I expected the letter that was to fix the date of my departure. Henry proposed a walking tour in the area around Ingolstadt. I agreed with pleasure to this. We passed two weeks in these rambles; my health and spirits had long come back to me, and they gained strength from the exercise. I became the same happy creature who, a few years ago, loved and beloved by all, had no sorrow or care.

We returned to our college on a Sunday afternoon; the peasants were dancing, and everyone we met appeared happy. My own spirits were high, and I bounded along with feelings of joy.

In my chambers I found the following letter from my father:

My dear Victor,

You have probably waited for a letter to fix the date of your return to us. How, Victor, can I relate our misfortune?

William is dead! That sweet child, whose smiles delighted and warmed my heart, who was so gentle, yet so happy! Victor, he is murdered!

Last Thursday (May 7th) I, my niece, and your two brothers went to walk in Plainpalais. The evening was warm, and we walked farther than usual. It was already dusk when we thought of returning, and then we discovered that William and Ernest, who had gone on before, were not to be found. So we rested on a seat to wait for them. Soon Ernest came and asked if we had seen his brother; he said that he had been playing with him, that William had run away to hide, and that he had looked for him and afterwards waited for him a long time, but he did not return.

This account rather alarmed us, and we continued to search for him until nightfall, when Elizabeth wondered if he might have returned to the house. He was not there. We returned again, with torches, for I could not rest at the thought that my sweet boy had become lost and was exposed to all the damps of night; Elizabeth also suffered with worry. At about five in the morning I discovered my lovely boy, whom the night before I had seen blooming and active, stretched on the grass, pale and motionless; the print of the murderer's fingers was on his neck.

He was brought home, and Elizabeth fainted. When she again had her wits, she wept. Come, dearest Victor; you alone can console Elizabeth. She weeps continually. We are all unhappy, but will not that be an additional reason for you, my son, to return and be our comforter?

Your affectionate and afflicted father,
Alphonse Frankenstein
Geneva, May 12, 17—

I motioned to Clerval to take up the letter while I walked up and down the room. Tears gushed from Clerval's eyes as he read the account of my misfortune.

"I can offer you no consolation, my friend," said he. "Your disaster cannot be fixed. What do you intend to do?"

"To go instantly to Geneva; come with me, Henry, to order the horses."

It was completely dark when I arrived on the outskirts of Geneva; the gates of the town were already
shut, and I had to pass the night at Secheron, a village
about a mile from the city. The sky was calm. Unable to
rest, I decided to visit the spot where my poor William
had been murdered. As I could not pass through the
town, I had to cross the lake in a boat to arrive at
Plainpalais. During this short voyage I saw the lightning
playing on the summit of Mont Blanc. The storm
appeared to approach rapidly. I soon felt the rain coming slowly in large drops.

While I watched the storm, I wandered on with a
hasty step. I then noticed in the gloom a figure that

In the storm, I noticed a figure hiding behind a clump of trees.

stole from behind a clump of trees near me; I stood fixed, gazing; I could not be mistaken. A flash of lightning lit up the object and showed its shape plainly to me; its gigantic stature and the deformity of its hideous face instantly showed me that it was the wretch, the filthy demon to whom I had given life. What was he doing there? Could he be the murderer of my brother? No sooner did the idea cross my mind than I became convinced of its truth; my teeth chattered, and I was forced to lean against a tree for support.

The figure passed me quickly, and I lost it in the gloom. Nothing in human shape could have destroyed that fair child. *He* was the murderer! I could not doubt it. I thought of chasing the devil, but it would have been in vain, for another flash showed him to me hanging among the rocks of the steep Mount Salève. He soon reached the summit and disappeared.

I remained motionless. The thunder stopped, but the rain still continued. I turned over in my mind the events that until now I had wanted to forget: the whole line of my progress toward the creation, the appearance of the work of my own hands alive at my bedside, and its leaving. Two years had now nearly gone by since the night on which he first received life, and was this his first crime? Alas! I had turned loose into the world a crazed wretch who delighted in bloodshed.

Day dawned and I walked toward the town. The gates were open, and I hurried to my father's house. My first thought was to reveal what I knew of the murderer and have him pursued. But I paused when I thought about the story that I had to tell. A being whom I myself had formed and brought to life had met me at midnight among the cliffs of a forbidding mountain. I well knew that if any other had told such a story to me, I should have looked upon it as the ravings of a madman.

Besides, the strange animal would escape any chase we made, if I were even believed. Who could arrest a creature capable of climbing the steep sides of Mount Salève? I decided to remain silent.

It was about five in the morning when I entered my father's house. I told the servants not to disturb the family and went into the library to wait.

I gazed at the picture of my mother, which stood over the mantelpiece. Below this picture was a miniature of William, and my tears flowed when I looked upon it. While I was weeping, Ernest entered.

"Welcome, my dearest Victor," said he. "Ah! I wish you had come three months ago, and then you would have found us all joyous. You come to us now to share a misery that nothing can help."

Tears fell from my brother's eyes.

My father entered. I saw unhappiness on his face, but he tried to welcome me cheerfully. We were soon joined by Elizabeth. Time had altered her since I last beheld her; it had given her loveliness finer than the beauty of her youthful years.

My father, on the other hand, noticed with pain the change in my face, and tried to give me strength.

"Do you think, Victor," said he, "that I do not suffer also? No one could love a child more than I loved your brother"—tears came into his eyes as he spoke—"but is it not a duty of the survivors that they should give up adding to the unhappiness by an appearance of too much grief? It is also a duty owed to yourself, for too much sorrow prevents you getting better."

5. Frankenstein Meets His Monster

SEVERAL DAYS LATER we went to our house at Belrive. This change was good for me. The shutting of the gates regularly at ten o'clock and the impossibility of remaining on the lake after that hour had made our living within the walls of Geneva very uncomfortable to me. I was now free. Often, after the rest of the family had gone to bed for the night, I took the boat and passed many hours on the water.

Sometimes, with my sails set, I was carried by the wind; and sometimes, after rowing into the middle of the lake, I left the boat to go its own way. I was often tempted, when all was at peace around me, to plunge into the silent lake, that the waters might close over me forever. But I held back when I thought of the heroic and suffering Elizabeth, whom I tenderly loved, and whose life was bound up with mine. I thought also of my father and surviving brother; should I, by departing this world, leave them exposed and unprotected to the violence of the fiend whom I had let loose among them?

There was always room for fear so long as anything I loved remained behind. My hatred of this fiend cannot be imagined.

Ours was a house of sadness. My father's health was poor. Elizabeth was no longer that happy creature who in earlier youth wandered with me on the banks of the lake and talked of our future.

"William was killed," said she, in agony, "and the mur-

36

derer has escaped. He walks about the world free, and perhaps respected."

I listened in pain to her words. I, not in deed but in effect, was the true murderer. Elizabeth saw the sadness in my face, and kindly taking my hand, she said, "My dearest friend, you must calm yourself. These events have affected me, God knows how deeply; but I am not so wretched as you are." Even as she spoke, I drew near to her, as if in terror, for fear that at that very moment the destroyer had been near to rob me of her.

Sometimes the passions of my soul drove me to seek, by exercise and by change of place, some relief from my feelings. It was during one such instance that I suddenly left my home and went off toward the near Alpine valleys to forget myself and my sorrows.

My wanderings took me toward the valley of Chamonix. I had visited it during my boyhood. Six years had passed since then: I was a wreck—but nothing had changed in those scenic views.

The weather was fine; it was about the middle of August, nearly two months since William's death. I went far into the ravine of Arve. I passed the bridge of Pellissier, where the ravine, which the river forms, opened before me, and I began to climb the mountain that overhangs it. Soon after that I entered the valley of Chamonix. The high and snow mountains were its boundaries. Immense glaciers approached the road; I heard the rumbling thunder of falling avalanches. Mont Blanc raised itself from the surrounding peaks, and its tremendous dome overlooked the valley.

At length I reached the village of Chamonix. For a short time I remained at the window in the inn watching the lightning that played above Mont Blanc and listening to the rushing of the Arve, which went its noisy way beneath.

I spent the following day roaming through the valley. The steep sides of vast mountains were before me; the icy wall of the glacier overhung me; a few pines were scattered around; and the silence was broken only by the thunder sound of the avalanche or the cracking of the ice. These scenes kept my mind from the thoughts over which I had brooded for the last month.

The next morning, the rain was pouring, and thick mists hid the tops of the mountains. But what were rain and storm to me? My mule brought me toward the top of Montanvert. The view of the tremendous and slowly moving glacier filled me with awe and joy.

The climb up was dangerously steep. In a thousand spots I was able to see the traces of the winter avalanche, where trees lay broken. The path, as I went along higher, was cut into by ravines of snow, down which stones continually rolled from above; one of them was particularly dangerous because the slightest sound, even a loud voice, might shake the air and cause a landslide of snow. I looked on the valley beneath; mists were rising from the rivers which ran through it, while rain poured from the dark sky.

It was nearly noon when I arrived at the top of the climb. For some time I sat upon the rock that overlooks the sea of ice. A mist covered both that and the mountains. Soon a breeze blew away the clouds, and I walked down into the glacier. The surface is very uneven, rising like the waves of a troubled sea, with deep gaps here and there. The field of ice is almost three miles wide, and I spent nearly two hours in crossing it. The opposite mountain is steep-cliffed rock. I stood upon it, gazing on Montanvert and Mont Blanc.

It was then that I beheld the figure of a man, at some distance, advancing toward me with great speed. He bounded over the gaps in the ice, among which I had

The figure of a man advanced toward me with great speed.

walked with care; his height and build, also, as he came, seemed to be more than that of a man.

I was troubled; a mist came over my eyes, and I felt faint. I saw, as the shape came nearer, that it was the wretch I had created. I trembled with rage and horror, deciding to wait for him and then fight with him in mortal combat. He approached; his face showed bitterness while his ugliness made him almost too horrible to look at.

"Devil," I said, "do you dare approach me? And don't you fear my vengeance? Go away, vile beast! Or rather, stay, so that I may trample you to dust!"

"I expected this greeting," said the demon. "All men hate the wretched; how, then, must I be hated, who am miserable beyond all living things! Yet you, my creator, hate and reject me, your creature, to whom you are bound by ties breakable only by the death of one of us. You propose to kill me. How dare you play in this way with life? Do your duty toward me, and I will do mine toward you and the rest of mankind. If you will go along with my conditions, I will leave them and you at peace; but if you refuse, I will kill your remaining friends."

"Hateful monster! You murderous fiend! The tortures of hell are too good for you! Wretched devil! You reproach me with creating you; come on, then, that I may kill the being I so thoughtlessly created."

I sprang at him, but he easily dodged me.

He said, "Be calm! I beg you to listen to me. Haven't I suffered enough? Life is dear to me, and I will defend it. Remember, you made me more powerful than yourself; my height is greater than yours, my muscles stronger. But I will not be tempted to fight you. I am your creature, and I will be mild and polite to my natural lord if you will also do your duty to me. Oh, Frankenstein, do not be fair to every other person and trample upon me alone, to whom your justice and affection is most due. Everywhere I see happiness, from which I alone am excluded. I was kind and good; misery made me a fiend. Make me happy, and I shall again be good."

"Go away! I will not listen to this. There can be no conversation between you and me; we are enemies. Go! Or let us fight to the death!"

"How can I persuade you to listen to me, your creature, who begs for your kindness and sympathy? Believe me, Frankenstein, I was good; my soul glowed with love; but am I not miserably alone? You, my creator, hate me; what hope can I gather from your fellow creatures, who owe me nothing? They spurn and hate me. The deserted mountains and icy glaciers are my refuge. I have wandered here many days; the caves of ice, which I do not fear, are a home to me, and the only one that mankind does not mind me having. If more people knew of me, they would do as you do and arm themselves for my destruction. Shall I not then hate them who hate me? Yet it is in your power to help me, and deliver them from my evil rage.

"Let your feelings be moved, and do not put me off. Listen to my story; when you have heard that, give me up or help me, as you shall judge that I deserve. But listen to me. The guilty are allowed, by human laws, to speak in their own defense before they are condemned.

"Frankenstein, you accuse me of murder, and yet you would destroy your own creature. Listen to me, and then, if you can, destroy the work of your hands."

"Cursed be the day, hated devil, in which you first saw light! Cursed be my hands that formed you! You have made me wretched beyond words. You have left me no power to think whether I am fair to you or not. Go! Relieve me from the sight of your detested face!"

"I relieve you this way, my creator," he said, and

placed his hands before my eyes, which I pushed away. "That is how I take from you a sight which you hate. Still you can listen to me with kindness. Hear my tale; it is long and strange, and the temperature of this place is not good for you; come to the hut upon the mountain. The sun is yet high in the heavens; before it goes down, you will have heard my story, and then you can decide. On you it rests whether I leave forever the world of men and lead a harmless life or become the murderer of your fellow creatures."

As he said this, he led the way across the ice; I followed. I decided at least to listen to his tale. We crossed the ice and climbed the opposite mountain. The air was cold, and the rain again began to fall; we went into his hut. I sat myself by the fire that my creature had lighted, and he began his story.

6. The Monster's Story

"IT IS VERY DIFFICULT to remember the first period of my life; all the events of that time appear confused. I saw, felt, heard, and smelled at the same time; and it was, indeed, a long time before I learned to tell my senses apart.

"I remember a strong light pressed upon my nerves, so that I had to shut my eyes. Darkness then came over me and troubled me, but hardly had I felt this when, by opening my eyes, the light poured in upon me again.

"I walked and went outside. I now found that I could wander wherever I liked. The light became more and more bothersome to me, and the heat tired me as I walked. I looked for a place where I could be in shade. There was a forest near Ingolstadt, and I lay by the side of a brook resting, until I felt tormented by hunger and thirst. I ate some berries which I found hanging on the trees or lying on the ground. I satisfied my thirst at the brook and then, lying down, was overcome by sleep.

"It was dark when I awoke; I felt cold also, and half frightened, finding myself so alone. Before I left your apartment, I had covered myself with some clothes, but these were not enough to keep me from the damp of night. I was a poor, helpless, miserable wretch; I knew nothing; but feeling pain come in on me from all sides, I sat down and wept.

"Soon a gentle light came over the heavens and gave me a feeling of pleasure. I started up and saw a radiant form rise from among the trees—the moon! I gazed with a kind of wonder. It moved slowly, but it lit up my path, and I again went out in search of berries. I was still cold when under one of the trees I found a huge cloak with which I covered myself, and I sat down upon the ground. I felt light and hunger and thirst and darkness; sounds rang in my ears, and on all sides various scents came to me; the only object that I could make out was the bright moon, and I fixed my eyes on that with pleasure.

"Several changes of day and night passed, and I began to tell my senses apart from one another. I gradually saw plainly the clear stream that supplied me with drink and the trees that shaded me with their leaves.

"I was delighted when I first discovered that a pleasant sound came from the throats of the little winged animals. Sometimes I tried to imitate the pleasant songs of the birds, but I was unable to. Sometimes I wished to express my feelings in my own way, but the sounds that broke from my mouth frightened me into silence again.

"The moon had disappeared from the night, and again, with a smaller form, showed itself while I still remained in the forest. My sensations had by this time become distinct, and every day my mind received more ideas. My eyes became accustomed to the light and to seeing objects in their right forms; I could tell insects from plants, and by degrees, one plant from another. I found that the sparrow uttered harsh songs, while those of the blackbird and thrush were sweet.

"One day, when I was cold, I found a fire that had been left by some wandering beggars, and I was overcome with delight at the warmth I drew from it. In my joy I thrust my hand into the live coals, but quickly drew it out again with a cry of pain.

"How strange, I thought, that the same cause should produce such opposite effects! I looked at the coals, and to my joy found them to be wood. I quickly collected some branches, but they were wet and would not burn. I was confused by this and sat still watching the fire. The wet wood I had placed near the heat dried and caught on fire. I thought about this and discovered the cause. When night came on and brought sleep with it, I was in the greatest fear that my fire should go out. I covered it carefully with dry wood and leaves and placed wet branches upon it; and then, spreading my cloak, I lay on the ground and sank into sleep.

"It was morning when I awoke, and my first care was to visit the fire. I uncovered it, and a gentle breeze quickly fanned it into a flame. I observed this also and made a fan of branches. When night came again I found, with pleasure, that the fire gave light as well as heat and that the discovery of this element was useful to me in my food, for I found some of the meat that the travelers had left had been roasted and tasted much better than the berries I gathered from the trees. I tried, then, to cook my food in the same manner, placing it on the live embers. I found that the berries were spoiled by this while the nuts and roots were much improved.

"Food, however, became hard to find, and I often spent the whole day searching for a few acorns. I decided to leave this place, to look for one where the few needs I had would be more easily satisfied. In leaving, however, I much regretted the loss of the fire, as I did not know how to make one.

"I wrapped myself up in my cloak and struck across the wood toward the setting sun. I passed three days in these rambles and finally discovered the open country. A great deal of snow had fallen the night before, and the fields were all white; I found my feet chilled by the cold, damp substance that covered the ground.

"It was about seven in the morning, and I longed to find food and shelter; at length I saw a small hut, which had doubtless been built for the shelter of some shepherd. This was a new sight to me, and I looked at the structure with great curiosity. Finding the door open, I entered. An old man sat in it near a fire, over which he was preparing his breakfast. He turned on hearing a noise and seeing me, shrieked loudly and ran out of the hut and across the fields. His flight somewhat surprised me. But I was enchanted by the appearance of the hut: here the snow and rain could not come; the ground was dry. I devoured the remains of the shepherd's breakfast, which was bread, cheese, and milk. Then, overcome by weariness, I lay down among some straw and fell asleep.

"It was noon when I awoke and, attracted by the warmth of the sun, which shone brightly on the white ground, I decided to begin again my travels; and, bringing along the remains of the peasant's breakfast in a bag I found, I set out across the fields for several hours, until at sunset I arrived at a village. I admired the huts, the cottages, the houses. The vegetables in the gardens and the milk and cheese that I saw placed in the windows of some of the cottages whetted my appetite.

"I entered one of these cottages, but I had hardly placed my foot within the door before the children shrieked, and one of the women fainted. The whole village was roused; some fled, some attacked me.

"Bruised by their stones, I escaped to the open country and took refuge in a low, bare shack. This shack, however, joined a cottage; after my bad experience in

"I entered one of the cottages, and the children shrieked."

the village, I dared not enter the cottage. My place of refuge was made of wood, but so low that I could barely sit upright in it. There was no floor but the earth itself, but it was dry. And although the wind poured through numerous cracks, I found it a pleasant shelter from the snow and rain, and still more from the cruelty of mankind.

"As soon as morning dawned, I crept out so that I might look at the cottage and find out if I could remain in my shelter. It was at the back of the cottage and surrounded on the sides by a pigsty and a clear pool of water. One side was open, and by that side I had crept in. I decided to live in this shack. It was a paradise compared to the forest.

"I ate my breakfast of bread, which I had stolen, and was about to go out and drink from the clear pool when I heard a step and, looking through a crack, I saw a young creature passing by with a pail on her head. The girl was young and gentle, yet she was poorly dressed, in a blue petticoat and cotton jacket. Her blonde hair was braided. I lost sight of her, and in about fifteen minutes she returned with the pail, which was now partly filled with milk. As she walked along, a young man met her. Uttering a few sounds, he took the pail from her head and brought it to the cottage himself. She followed, and they disappeared.

"Soon I saw the young man again, with some tools in his hand, crossing the field behind the cottage; and the girl was also busy, sometimes in the house and sometimes in the yard.

"On looking at my shack, I found that one of the windows of the cottage had once looked out in its direction, but the panes had been filled up with wood. In one

The young girl listened as the silver-haired old man played the guitar.

of these pieces of wood was a small crack through which I could peek. Through this crack a small room was visible; it was clean but very bare of furniture. In one corner, near a small fire, sat a silver-haired old man, leaning his head on his hands. The young girl was busy in cleaning up the cottage; but soon she took something out of a drawer, which she worked with her hands, and she sat down beside the old man, who, taking up an instrument, began to play and make sounds sweeter than the voice of the nightingale. It was a lovely sight, even to me, who had never seen anything beautiful before.

"The old man played a sweet, sad song that drew tears from the eyes of the girl; the old man took no notice of this until she sobbed. He then said a few words, and the girl, leaving her work, knelt at his feet.

"He raised her and smiled with such kindness and affection that I felt sensations of a strange and overpowering nature; they were a mixture of pain and pleasure, such as I had never before felt, either from hunger or cold, warmth or food; and I left the window unable to bear these feelings.

"Soon after this the young man returned with a load of wood. The girl met him at the door and took some of the wood into the cottage and placed it on the fire; then the young man showed her a large loaf of bread and a piece of cheese. She seemed pleased and went into the garden for some roots and plants, which she placed in water and then upon the fire. She then continued her work while the young man went into the garden and dug up roots. After he had done this for an hour, the young woman joined him, and they entered the cottage together.

"They all sat down to eat. The meal was quickly over. The young woman again cleaned up the cottage, and the old man walked in front of the cottage in the sun for a few minutes, leaning on the arm of the young man. The old man returned to the cottage, and the young man, with tools different from those he had used in the morning, went out across the fields.

"Night quickly came on, but to my wonder, I found that the cottagers had a way of keeping the light by the use of candles and I was delighted to find that the setting of the sun did not put an end to the pleasure I had in watching my human neighbors.

"In the evening the young girl and the young man were busy in tasks I did not understand; and the old man again took up the instrument which made the divine sounds that had enchanted me in the morning. As soon as he had finished, the youth began, not to play, but to say words while the others listened; I since found that he was reading aloud, but at that time I knew nothing of speaking or reading.

"The family, after having done this for a short time, put out their lights and went to bed. The cottagers arose the next morning before the sun. The young woman fixed up the cottage and prepared the food, and the youth went out.

"This day passed in the same way as the first. The young man was busy out of doors, and the girl indoors. The old man, whom I soon saw to be blind, spent his time on his instrument or in thought.

"A long period passed before I realized that this family was suffering poverty. Their food consisted entirely of the vegetables of their garden and the milk of one cow, which gave very little during the winter. Several times the younger people placed food before the old man and had none for themselves.

"This kindness moved me. I had been accustomed, during the night, to stealing a part of their food for myself, but when I found that in doing this I deprived the cottagers, I stopped and satisfied myself with berries, nuts, and roots, which I gathered from a near-by forest. I found also another way through which I was able to help them. The youth spent a great part of each day in collecting wood for the family fire, and during the night I often took his tools and brought home enough firewood for several days.

"I remember that when I did this for the first time, the young woman, upon opening the door in the morning, appeared greatly surprised to see a pile of wood. She uttered some words in a loud voice, and the youth joined her and also expressed surprise. I observed, with pleasure, that he did not go to the forest that day but spent it in repairing the cottage and gardening.

"Slowly I made a more important discovery. I found that these people had a way of telling about their experience and feelings to one another by making sounds. I noticed that the words they spoke sometimes brought pleasure or pain, smiles or sadness, in the hearers. This was a godlike talent, and I wanted to learn it. But I found it too difficult. They spoke quickly, and the words they uttered, not having any apparent connection with visible objects, meant nothing to me.

"By great study, however, and after having spent several months there, I began to see that the names were given to some of the most familiar objects of conversation; I learned and used some of the words: 'fire,' 'milk,' 'bread,' and 'wood.' I also learned the names of the cottagers themselves. The youth and the girl had each of them several names, but the old man had only one, which was 'father.' The girl was called 'sister' or 'Agatha,' and the youth 'Felix,' 'brother,' or 'son.' I cannot describe the delight I felt when I learned the ideas for these sounds and was able to pronounce them. I made out several other words without being able as yet to understand or use them, such as 'good,' 'dearest,' 'unhappy.'

"I spent the winter in this way. The gentle manners and beauty of the cottagers greatly endeared them to me; when they were unhappy, I felt depressed; when they rejoiced, I felt joy.

*Felix picked the first little white flower
from the snowy ground for his sister.*

"In the midst of their poverty, Felix carried with pleasure to his sister the first little white flower that peeped out from beneath the snowy ground. Early in the morning, before she had risen, he cleared away the snow on her path to the milk house, drew water from the well, and brought the wood from the shed, where, to his surprise, he found his wood supply always replenished by an invisible hand. In the day, I believe, he worked sometimes for a neighboring farmer, because he often went out and did not return until dinner, yet brought no wood with him. At other times he worked in the garden, but as there was little to do in the frosty season, he read to the old man and Agatha.

"This reading had puzzled me very much at first, but by degrees I discovered that he uttered many of the same sounds when he read as when he talked. I guessed, therefore, that he recognized on the paper signs for speech, and I longed to understand these also; but how was that possible when I did not even understand the sounds for which they stood as signs?

"I longed to introduce myself to the cottagers, but I knew I ought not to do so until I had first become master of their language, which might help them overlook the deformity of my face and body.

"I had admired the perfect appearances of my cottagers—their grace, beauty, and delicate complexions; but how terrified I was when I viewed myself in the water outside! At first I started back, unable to believe that it was indeed I who was reflected in the pool; and when I became convinced that I was the monster that I am, I was filled with sadness and horror.

"As the sun became warmer and the light of day longer, the snow vanished, and I looked at the bare trees and the dark earth. From this time Felix was busier, and their hunger disappeared. Their food was hearty and wholesome, and they had enough of it. Several new kinds of plants sprang up in the garden. The old man, leaning on his son, walked each day at noon if it did not rain, as I found it was called when the sky poured forth its water.

"My life in the shack was always the same. During the morning I watched the actions of the cottagers, and when they went to their various chores, I slept; I spent the remainder of the day in watching my friends. When they went to bed, if there was any moon or if the night was starlit, I went into the woods and gathered my own food and fuel for the cottage. When I returned, I cleared their path of the snow and did those chores I had seen done by Felix. These chores made them wonder about the 'good spirit' who had helped them.

"I imagined presenting myself to them. I imagined that they would be disgusted until, by my gentle manner and kind words, I should first win their favor and afterwards their love. Although my voice was very unlike the soft music of their tones, yet I pronounced such words as I understood with some ease.

"Spring came rapidly; the weather became fine and the skies cloudless. It surprised me that what before was barren and gloomy should now bloom with the most beautiful flowers and greenery. My senses were refreshed. It was on one of these days, when my cottagers were resting from their labor—the old man played on his guitar, and the children listened to him—that someone tapped at the door.

"It was a lady on horseback. She was dressed in a dark suit and covered with a black veil. Agatha asked a question, to which the stranger only replied by saying, in a sweet accent, the name of Felix. On hearing this word, Felix came up to to the lady, who, when she saw him, pulled up her veil. Her hair was shining black and strangely braided; her eyes were dark but gentle.

"Felix was delighted when he saw her. She wiped a few tears from her lovely eyes, held out her hand to him, and he kissed it. He called her his sweet Arabian. She did not seem to understand him, but smiled. He helped her down from the horse and brought her into the cottage. Some conversation took place between him and his father, and the young stranger knelt at the old man's feet and would have kissed his hand, but he raised her and hugged her.

"I soon noticed that although the stranger uttered sounds and appeared to have a language of her own, she neither understood nor was understood by the cottagers. They made many signs that I did not understand, but I saw that she brought gladness to the cottage. Soon, I found, by the hearing of the same sound, which the stranger repeated after them, that she was trying to learn their language; and the idea instantly occurred to me that I should make use of the same instructions to learn it as well. The stranger learned about twenty words at the first lesson; most of them were those that I had already acquired. As night came on, Agatha and the Arabian went to bed early. Felix kissed the hand of the stranger and said, 'Good night, sweet Safie.'

"She and I improved rapidly in the knowledge of the language, so that in two months I began to understand most of the words uttered by my cottagers. In the meantime, my nightly rambles were an extreme pleasure to me, although they were shortened by the late setting and early rising of the sun; I never went out during daylight, fearful of meeting with the same treatment I had formerly endured in the first village I entered.

"I spent my days in close attention in order to master the language more quickly. I understood and could imitate almost every word they spoke. While I improved in speech, I also learned how to read, since it was taught to the stranger, and this opened before me a wide field for wonder and delight. Lessons were impressed upon me deeply. I heard of the difference of sexes, and the birth and growth of children, how the father loved the smiles of the baby, how all the life and cares of the mother were wrapped up in the child; how the mind of youth expanded and gained knowledge; of brother, sister, and all the various relationships that bind one human being to another.

"But where were my friends and relations? No father had watched my first days, no mother had blessed me with smiles and kisses; or if they had, all my past life was now a blot, which I could not remember. From my earliest remembrance I had been as I then was in height and appearance. I had never yet seen a being resembling me or who claimed any relationship with me. What was I?"

7. The Monster's Rage

"ONE NIGHT IN the beginning of August, during my usual visit to the neighboring wood where I collected my own food and brought home firewood for the cottagers, I found on the ground a leather bag containing several pieces of clothing and some books. I eagerly picked it up and returned with it to my shack. Fortunately the books were written in the language which I had learned from my neighbors. They gave me extreme delight. I read and studied them while my friends were busy with their chores.

"As I read, I reflected on my own feelings and life. I found myself similar yet at the same time strangely unlike the beings about whom I read and watched. I was hideous and my body was gigantic. What did this mean? Who was I? What was I? Where did I come from? These questions continually came to me, but I was unable to answer them.

"Soon after my arrival in the shack, I had discovered some papers in the pocket of the coat that I had taken from your laboratory. At first I had not looked at them, but now that I was able to read, I began to study them. It was your journal of the four months that led up to my creation. You described in these papers every step you took in the progress of your work; this account was mingled with stories of your life. You doubtless remem-

57

ber these papers. Here they are. All the details are told of my creation, in language that showed your horror. I sickened as I read.

"'Hateful day when I came to life!' I exclaimed in agony. 'You cursed creator! Why did you make a monster so hideous that even *you* turned from me in disgust?' These were my thoughts.

"But when I thought about the goodness of the cottagers, I persuaded myself that when they began to know my own goodness, they would feel for me and overlook my ugliness. Could they turn from their door one, however monstrous, who asked for their kindness and friendship?

"Autumn passed in this way. With surprise and grief I saw the leaves fall, and nature again become barren and bleak. But I turned with more attention toward the cottagers. The more I saw of them, the greater became my hopes of gaining their friendship.

"The winter came on, and an entire cycle of the seasons had taken place since I awoke into life. I finally decided to enter the cottage when the blind man should be alone. I had wisdom enough to know that my ugliness was the cause of the horror of those who had seen me. My voice, although rough, had nothing terrible in it; I thought, therefore, that if in the absence of the children I could gain the good will of the old man, I might by his support be tolerated by the younger ones.

"One day, when the sun shone on the red leaves that had fallen over the ground, Safie, Agatha, and Felix went out on a long walk, and the old man, at his own wish, was left alone in the cottage. When his children had left, he took up his guitar and played several sad, sweet songs. Finally, laying aside the instrument, he sat thinking.

"My heart beat quickly; this was the hour and

moment of truth, which would satisfy my hopes or prove my fears. All was silent in and around the cottage; it was an excellent opportunity.

"I left the shack and approached the door of their cottage. I knocked. 'Who is there?' said the old man. 'Come in.'

"I entered. 'Pardon me,' said I; 'I am a traveler in need of a little rest; you would greatly help me if you would allow me to remain a few minutes before the fire.'

"'Enter,' he said, 'and I will try in what way I can to help you; but, unluckily, my children are out, and as I am blind, I am afraid I shall find it hard to provide some food for you.'

"'Do not trouble yourself, my kind host; I have food; it is warmth and rest only that I need. I am an unfortunate creature; I look around and I have no family or friend upon earth.'

"'Do not despair. To be friendless is indeed unfortunate, but the hearts of men are often full of brotherly love and kindness. Be hopeful. If you will tell me your story, I perhaps may be able to help you. I am blind, and cannot judge your face, but there is something in your words that tells me that you are honest. I am poor and living far from my homeland, but it will give me pleasure to help a human creature.'

"'Excellent man! I thank you and accept your generous offer. You raise me from the dust by this kindness; and I trust that, by your help, I shall not be driven from the society and kindness of your fellow creatures.'

"'Heaven forbid!'

"'How can I thank you, my best and only friend? From your lips I have heard the voice of kindness; I shall be forever grateful.' I sank on the chair and sobbed aloud. At that moment I heard the steps of the young cottagers. I had not a moment to lose, but seizing the hand of the old man, I cried, 'Now is the time! Save and protect me! Do not desert me!'

"'Great God!' exclaimed the old man. 'Who are you?'

"At that instant the cottage door was opened, and Felix, Safie, and Agatha entered. Who can describe their horror on seeing me? Agatha fainted, and Safie rushed out of the cottage. Felix darted forward, and tore me

Felix darted forward, tearing me from his father,
and struck me with a stick.

from his father, to whose knees I clung, and struck me with a stick. I could have torn him limb from limb, but I kept myself from doing so. I saw him about to attack me again, when I left the cottage and escaped, unnoticed, to my shack.

"Cursed, cursed creator! Why did I live?

"When night came, I left the shack and wandered in the wood; and now, no longer worried about being found out, I let out, in my agony, fearful howlings. Oh!

What a miserable night I passed! There were no men that existed who would pity or help; and should I feel kindness toward my enemies? No; from that moment I declared everlasting war against mankind, and more than all, against him who had created me.

"The sun rose; I heard the voices of men and knew that it was impossible to return to my shack during that day. I hid myself in thick underbrush. That night, I crept out from my hiding place and went in search of food. When I had gathered enough, I went back to the cottage. All there was at peace. I crept into my shack and awaited morning. But even after the sun mounted high in the heavens, still the cottagers did not appear. Where were they? Soon I saw, outside, Felix and another man approach.

"'We can never again live in this cottage,' said Felix. 'The life of my father is in the greatest danger, owing to the dreadful event I have told you. My wife and my sister will never recover from their horror.'

"Felix and his companion entered the cottage, in which they remained for only a few minutes, and then left. I never saw any of the family again.

"I continued for the remainder of the day in my shack. My cottagers had left and had broken the only link that held me to the world. For the first time the feelings of revenge and hatred filled my heart, and I did not try to control them. As night came on, I placed firewood and straw around the cottage, and after having destroyed the garden, I waited until the moon had gone down to begin my task.

"I lighted the dry branch of a tree and danced with fury around the cottage. I lit the straw. The wind fanned the fire, and the cottage was quickly covered in flames.

"I decided to go far away from there. The thought of you, Frankenstein, crossed my mind. I learned from your papers that you were my father, my creator; and to whom could I go to but you? Among the lessons Felix had given Safie was geography. You had mentioned Geneva as the name of your native town, and toward this place I decided to go. I possessed a map of the country.

"I traveled only at night, fearful of meeting a human being. Nature decayed around me, and the sun became heatless; rain and snow poured around me; mighty rivers were frozen; the surface of the earth was hard and bare, and I found no shelter. The nearer I approached your city, the more deeply did I feel the spirit of revenge. I arrived on the outskirts of Switzerland when the sun had recovered its warmth and the earth again began to look green.

"One morning, finding that my path lay through a deep wood, I decided to continue my journey after the sun had risen. I wound among the paths of the wood, until I came to its edge, which was bounded by a deep and rapid river. Here I paused, not exactly knowing what path to take, when I heard the sound of voices, which led me to hide myself in the shade of a tree.

"I was scarcely concealed when a young girl came running toward the spot where I was hidden, laughing, as if she ran from someone in play. She went on along the steep sides of the river, when suddenly her foot slipped, and she fell into the rapid water. I rushed from my hiding place and into the powerful current, and saved her and dragged her to shore. I was suddenly interrupted by the approach of a peasant, who was probably the person from whom she had playfully fled. On seeing me, he darted toward me and tearing the girl from my arms, hurried away toward the deeper parts of the wood. I followed, I hardly knew why; but when the man saw me draw near, he aimed a gun at me and fired.

I sank to the ground, and the gunman, with more speed, went on into the wood.

"This was then the reward of my kindness! I had saved a human being from death, and as a result I now was wounded by a bullet. The feeling of kindness and gentleness which I had had a few moments before gave way to rage. The agony of my wound, however, overcame me, and I fainted.

"For some weeks I led a miserable life in the woods, trying to cure the wound which I had received. When it did heal, I continued my journey, and two months later I reached Geneva.

"It was evening when I arrived, and I found a hiding place among the fields that surround the city. I was wondering how I should approach you when I was disturbed by a beautiful child who came running into the spot where I had chosen. Suddenly, as I gazed on him, an idea came upon me that this little creature had lived too short a time to be horrified by my ugliness. If, therefore, I could stop him and show him that I was friendly, I should not be so lonely.

"I caught the boy as he passed. As soon as he saw me, he placed his hands over his eyes and screamed. I drew his hands away, and said, 'Child, what is the meaning of this? I do not mean to hurt you; listen to me.'

"He struggled and cried, 'Let me go, monster! Ugly wretch! You wish to eat me and tear me to pieces. You are a beast. Let me go, or I will tell my papa.'

"'Boy, you will never see your father again; you must come with me.'

"'Hideous monster! Let me go. My papa is an important man! He is Mister Frankenstein—he will punish you. You dare not keep me.'

"'Frankenstein! You belong then to the family of my

"The child struggled and I grasped his throat to silence him."

enemy—toward whom I have sworn eternal revenge; you shall be my first victim.'

"The child struggled and called me names; I grasped his throat to silence him, and in a moment he lay dead at my feet.

"I gazed on my victim, and my heart swelled with triumph; clapping my hands, I exclaimed, 'I, too, can create misery; my enemy can be hurt; this death will bring despair to him, and a thousand other miseries shall torment and destroy him.'

"For some days I haunted the spot where these scenes had taken place, sometimes wishing to see you, sometimes deciding to leave the world and its miseries forever. At length I wandered toward these mountains and have climbed over them, consumed by a burning passion that you alone can satisfy. We may not part until you have promised to do what I ask. I am alone and miserable; mankind will not accept me; but a female creature as ugly and horrible as I am would accept me. My companion must be of the same type and have the same defects. This being you must create."

8. The Monster's Bride

THE MONSTER FINISHED speaking and fixed his gaze upon me, awaiting my reply. As I remained silent, he continued, "You must create a female for me with whom I can live. I demand it of you, and you must not refuse."

"I do refuse," I said, "and no torture shall ever make me agree to do it. Shall I create another like yourself, so that your joint wickedness might destroy the world? Go away! I have answered you; you may torture me, but I will never consent."

"You are in the wrong," replied the fiend, "and instead of threatening, I am content to reason with you. I am wicked because I am miserable.

"Am I not shunned and hated by all mankind? If I cannot gain love, I will cause fear. Beware; I will work at your destruction. What I ask of you is reasonable; I demand a creature of another sex, but as hideous as I; this is little enough, but it shall content me. It is true, we shall be monsters, cut off from all the world; but on that account we shall be more attached to each other. Our lives will not be happy, but they will be harmless and free from the misery I now feel. Oh! My creator, make me happy; let me give thanks to you! Let me see that you have some feeling for me; do not deny me my request!"

I was moved. I thought there was some justice in his argument. His story and the feelings he now expressed

65

proved him to be a creature of fine sensations, and did I not as his maker owe him all the portion of happiness that it was in my power to give him?

He saw my change of feeling and went on. "If you agree, neither you nor any other human being shall ever see us again; I will go to the vast wilds of South

"Am I not shunned and hated by all mankind?
Do not deny me my request!"

America. My food is not that of man; I do not destroy animals for my appetite; acorns and berries give me enough. My companion will be the same. We shall make our bed of dried leaves; the sun will shine on us as on mankind and will ripen our food. The picture I present to you is peaceful and human, and you must feel that you could deny it only out of cruelty."

His words had a strange effect upon me. I felt sorry for him and sometimes felt a wish to help him, but when I looked at him, when I saw the disgusting beast who moved and talked, my heart sickened and my feelings changed to those of horror and hatred. I tried to control these feelings.

After a long pause I decided that justice due to him and my fellow humans demanded of me that I should go along with his request. I said, "I consent to your demand, on your promise that you will leave Europe forever, and every other place where men live, as soon as I shall deliver into your hands a female who will go with you in your exile."

"I swear," he cried, "by the sun and by the blue sky of heaven and by the fire of love that burns in my heart, that if you grant my prayer, you shall never see me again. Return to your home and begin your work; I shall watch your progress; when you are ready, I shall appear."

Saying this, he quickly left me, fearful, perhaps, of my changing my mind. I saw him go down the mountain with greater speed than the flight of an eagle.

His story had taken the whole day, and the sun was upon the edge of the horizon when he left. Morning dawned before I arrived at the village of Chamonix; I took no rest but returned immediately to Geneva.

Day after day, week after week passed away on my return to Geneva. I found that I could not make a female without again devoting several months to study and calculations. I had heard of some discoveries made by an English scientist, the knowledge of which would be helpful to my work, and I decided to ask my father for permission to visit England.

I did not want to work on this creature while in my father's house. I knew that a thousand fearful accidents might occur, the slightest of which would horrify everyone. I must leave all those people I loved while working.

Once begun, the project would quickly be carried out, and then I might return to my family in peace and happiness. My promise fulfilled, the monster would go away forever.

My father, however, insisted that I go with a companion, my friend Clerval. This interfered with my plans, yet I agreed. To England, therefore, I was bound, and it was understood that my marriage with Elizabeth should take place immediately on my return.

It was at the end of September that I left Switzerland with Clerval. Alas, how great was the contrast between our feelings! He was alive to every new scene, joyful when he saw the beauties of the setting sun, while I, a miserable wretch, was haunted by a promise that kept me from enjoying anything.

At length we arrived in London. After passing several months in this wonderful and famous city, we received a letter from a person in Scotland who had formerly been our visitor at Geneva. He mentioned the beauties of his native country and asked us to journey as far north as Perth, where he lived. Clerval eagerly accepted this invitation, and I agreed to go along.

I packed up my chemical instruments and the materials I had collected, deciding to finish my work in some out-of-the-way nook in the northern highlands of Scotland.

We left London on the 27th of March. I was not sorry. I had not worked to fulfill my promise for some time, and I feared the effects of the demon's disappointment. He might remain in Switzerland and avenge himself on my relatives. This idea tormented me. I waited for letters with impatience; if they were delayed, I was overcome by a thousand fears. Sometimes I thought that the fiend followed me and might punish my tardiness by murdering my friend Clerval. Because of this I told

Clerval that I wished to make the tour of Scotland alone. "You go and enjoy yourself," I said. "I may be gone for a month or two; but do not interfere with my travels, I beg you. Leave me at peace for a short while, and when I return, I hope it will be with a lighter heart."

Having parted from my friend, I decided to visit some remote spot of Scotland to finish my work alone. I did not doubt that the monster followed me and would know when I had finished.

I crossed the northern highlands and chose one of the most distant of the Orkney Islands as the scene of my labors. It was a place fitted for such work, being hardly more than a rock whose high sides were beaten upon by the waves. The soil was barren, with hardly enough pasture for the few cows and barely enough oatmeal for its natives, which consisted of five people. Vegetables and bread, and even fresh water, had to be brought from the mainland, which was about five miles away.

On the whole island there were but three miserable huts, and one of these was empty when I arrived. This I rented. It contained but two rooms, and these were poor. The thatch roof had fallen in, the walls were unplastered, and the door was off its hinges. I ordered it to be repaired, bought some furniture, and moved in.

In this hut I devoted the morning to labor; but in the evening, when the weather permitted, I walked on the stony beach of the sea to listen to the waves as they roared and dashed at my feet. I thought of Switzerland; it was far different from this lonely and barren landscape.

As I went on with my work, it became every day more horrible and disgusting to me. Sometimes I could not get myself to enter my laboratory for several days, and at other times I worked day and night in order to complete my work. It was, indeed, a filthy job. My heart was often sickened at the work of my hands.

I grew restless and nervous. Every moment I feared to meet the demon. In the meantime I worked on, and my labor was already far along. I looked toward its completion with hope.

I sat one evening in my laboratory; the sun had set, and the moon was just rising from the sea. Three years before, I had been working in just this way and had created a fiend whose barbarity had filled my heart with remorse. I was now about to form another being whose character I also did not know; she might become ten thousand times more evil than her mate and delight, for its own sake, in murder and violence. He had sworn to leave civilization and hide himself away, but she had not; and she, who in all probability was to become a thinking and reasoning animal, might refuse to go along with an agreement made before her creation. They might even hate each other; the creature who already lived hated his own ugliness, and might he not have a greater horror of it when it came before his eyes in the female form? She also might turn with disgust from him to the superior beauty of man; she might leave him, and he might be alone again, more angry than ever for having been spurned by one of his own kind.

Even if they were to leave Europe and live in the new world, one of the first results of their love would be children, and a race of devils would be born upon the earth who might terrorize mankind. Had I a right, for my own benefit, to put his curse upon future generations?

I trembled and my heart failed within me when, on looking up, I saw by the light of the moon the demon at the window. A ghastly grin wrinkled his lips as he gazed on me. Yes, he had followed me in my travels; he had

I saw the demon at the window, and a ghastly grin wrinkled his lips.

waited in forests, hid himself in caves, or taken refuge in the heaths; and he now came to check on my progress and claim the fulfillment of my promise.

As I looked on him, I thought I had to have been mad to promise to create another being like him, and I suddenly tore to pieces the monster on which I was working. The wretch saw me destroy the creature on whose future life he depended for happiness, and with a howl he ran off.

I left the room and, locking the door, made a vow never to begin again my labors. Several hours passed as I sat in the next room at the window gazing on the sea; it was almost motionless, for the winds were hushed. A few fishing boats alone specked the water, and now and then the gentle breeze brought the sound of voices as the fishermen called to one another.

In a few minutes I heard the creaking of my door. soon I heard the sound of footsteps along the passage; the door opened, and the wretch whom I dreaded appeared. Shutting the door, he approached me and said, "You have destroyed the work which you began. do you dare to break your promise? I have suffered hard and long; I left Switzerland with you; I crept along after you through Europe and across England. Do you dare to destroy my hopes?"

"Leave me!" I cried. "I do break my promise; I will never create another like you, equal in monstrousness."

"Remember that I have power; you believe yourself miserable, but I can make you so wretched that the light of day will be hateful to you. You are my creator, but I am your master; obey!"

"Your threats cannot move me to do an act of wickedness. Shall I, in cold blood, set loose upon the earth a demon whose delight is death and violence? Go away!"

"Shall each man," cried he, "find a wife, and each beast have his mate, and I be alone? I had feelings of affection, and they were met by hatred and scorn. Are you to be happy while I grovel in wretchedness? You can frustrate my other passions, but revenge remains! I may die, but first you shall curse the sun that gazes on your misery. Beware, for I am fearless and therefore powerful. I will watch with the cunning of a snake, that I may sting with its venom. You shall be sorry!"

"Devil, stop these words. I have declared my decision to you, and I am no coward to bend to your threats. Leave me; there is no changing my mind."

"Then I shall go; but remember, I shall be with you on your wedding night."

I started and exclaimed, "Villain! Before you threaten my life, be sure that you are yourself safe."

I would have grabbed him, but he escaped and fled the house. In a few minutes I saw him in his boat, which shot across the waters and was soon beyond my sight.

The night passed away, and the sun rose from the ocean; my feelings grew calmer. I left the house, the horrid scene of last night's dispute, and walked on the beach. I saw a fishing boat land close to me, and one of the men brought me a packet; it contained letters from Geneva, and one from Clerval asking me to leave my deserted island and to meet him at Perth so that we might go on southward together. This letter brought me back to life, and I decided to leave the island at the end of two days.

Yet before I left, there was a task to do; I must pack up my chemical instruments. The next morning, I unlocked the door of my laboratory. The remains of the half-finished creature, whom I had destroyed, lay scattered on the floor. With trembling hands, I brought the instruments out of the room, but then I realized that I ought not to leave the remains of my work to horrify the peasants; and so I put them into a basket, with a large number of stones, determined to throw them into the sea that very night.

Between two and three in the morning, the moon rose; and I then, putting my basket aboard a little rowboat, sailed out about four miles from the shore and cast my basket into the sea. I listened to the gurgling sound as it sank and then sailed away from the spot. I heard only the sound of the boat as it cut through the waves; this murmur lulled me, and in a short time I slept soundly.

I do not know how long I remained in this sleep, but when I awoke I found that the sun had already climbed into the sky. I steered my course toward the land. I saw boats near the shore and found myself suddenly transported back to the neighborhood of civilized man. Several people crowded toward the spot where I landed. They seemed very surprised at my appearance.

"My good friends," said I, "will you be so kind as to tell me the name of this town and tell me where I am?"

"In the town of Tervalon, where a murder was committed last night," said an elderly, well-dressed man.

I was introduced to the elderly man, who was the mayor. A fisherman, he told me, had reported that he had been out fishing the night before with his son and brother-in-law, James Cahill, when they landed at a creek about two miles below. The fisherman walked on

By the light of the lantern, they found the body of a dead man.

first, and his companions followed him. As he was walking along the sands, he struck his foot against something and fell on the ground. His companions came up to help him, and by the light of their lantern they found that he had fallen on the body of a man who was, to all appearances, dead. The first guess was that it was the corpse of some person who had been drowned and was thrown on shore by the waves, but on examination they found that the clothes were not wet and even that the body was not yet cold. They instantly carried it to the cottage of an old woman near the spot and tried to restore it to life. It appeared to be a handsome man, about twenty-five years old. He had apparently been strangled, for there was no sign of any violence except the mark of fingers on his neck.

When the mark of the fingers was mentioned, I remembered the murder of my brother and felt myself trembling. The mayor asked if I would go into the room where the body lay for burial. I entered the room and was led up to the coffin. When I saw the lifeless form of Henry Clerval stretched before me, I gasped for breath and collapsed.

9. Frankenstein's Wedding

FOR THE NEXT two months I lay in a fever, on the point of death. At this time my father traveled from Geneva to my side. In my first words to him, I said, "Are you, then, safe—and Elizabeth—and Ernest?"

My father calmed me with news of their welfare and said, "You traveled to England to find happiness, but death seems to follow you. And poor Clerval—"

The name of my poor murdered friend brought tears to my eyes, and we wept for several minutes.

My father was my good angel, however, and I gradually recovered my health. I was allowed to return to my native country.

It was necessary, indeed, that I should return without delay to Geneva so that I might watch over the lives of those I loved and lie in wait for the murderer.

On our voyage by ship, I passed through, in my memory, my whole life—my quiet happiness while living with my family in Geneva, the death of my mother, and my departure for Ingolstadt. I remembered, shuddering, the madness that hurried me on to the creation of my hideous enemy, and I called to mind the night in which he first lived. I wept bitterly.

The voyage came to an end. We landed and went on to Paris. A few days before we left Paris on our way to Switzerland, I received the following letter from Elizabeth:

My dear Victor,

It gave me the greatest pleasure to receive a letter from my uncle dated at Paris; you are no longer at a far distance, and I may hope to see you in less than two weeks. My poor cousin, how much you must have suffered! I expect to see you looking even more ill than when you left Geneva. This winter has been passed most miserably, yet I hope to find that peace is in your heart.

You well know, Victor, that our marriage had been the favorite plan of your parents ever since our childhood. We were told this when young and taught to look forward to it as an event that would certainly take place. We were fond playmates during childhood and, I believe, dear and valued friends to each other as we grew older. But as brother and sister often have a fondness toward each other without wanting to be married, may not such also be our case? tell me, dearest Victor. Answer me, I beg you, with simple truth—do you not love another?

You have traveled; you have spent several years of your life at Ingolstadt; and I confess to you, my friend, that when I saw you last autumn so unhappy, I could not help supposing that you might regret our engagement and believe yourself bound in honor to fulfill the wishes of your parents. I confess to you, my friend, that I love you and that in my airy dreams of the future you have been my constant friend and companion. But it is your happiness I want as well as my own when I declare to you that our marriage would make me miserable unless it were of your own free choice.

Do not let this letter disturb you; do not answer tomorrow or the next day or even until you come if it will give you pain. My uncle will send me news of your health, and if I see but one smile on your lips when we meet, I shall need no other happiness.

Elizabeth
Geneva, May 18, 17—

This letter revived in my memory what I had before forgotten, the threat of the fiend: *"I shall be with you on your wedding night!"* On that night would the demon try to destroy me and tear me from any little happiness that promised to relieve my sufferings. On that night he had determined to kill me. Well, so be it; a deadly struggle would take place: if he were victorious, I should be at peace and his power over me be at an end; if he were defeated, I should be a free man.

I wrote to Elizabeth. My letter was calm and affectionate. "I fear, my beloved girl," I said, "little happiness remains for us on earth; yet all that I may one day enjoy is centered in you. Chase away your fears; to you alone do I dedicate my life."

In about a week after the arrival of Elizabeth's letter, we returned to Geneva. The sweet girl welcomed me with warm affection, yet tears were in her eyes as she saw how illness had touched me.

Soon after our arrival my father spoke of my marriage to Elizabeth, asking when it would be. When I looked confused, he asked, "What, have you fallen in love with someone else?"

I replied, "I love Elizabeth and look forward to our union with delight. Let the day therefore be fixed; and I will dedicate myself to the happiness of my cousin."

I therefore arranged with my father that if my cousin would agree, the ceremony should take place in ten days.

Great God! If for one instant I had thought what might be the hellish intention of my fiendish enemy, I would rather have run away forever from my native country and wandered a friendless outcast over the earth than have consented to this marriage. But the monster had blinded me to his real intentions; and when I thought that I had prepared only my own death, I brought on that of a far dearer victim.

Preparations were made for the event, congratulatory visits were made, and all wore smiles. It was agreed that immediately after our weddings we should proceed to Villa Lavenza and spend our first days of happiness beside the beautiful lake near which it stood.

In the meantime I took every precaution to defend myself in case the fiend should openly attack me. I carried pistols and a dagger with me constantly and was ever on the watch to prevent him from taking me by surprise.

Elizabeth seemed happy; my calmness helped greatly to relieve her worries. But on the day that was to fulfill my wishes and my fate, she was sad, and a feeling of dread came over her; and perhaps she also thought of

After the wedding, Elizabeth and I began our journey by water.

"a terrible secret" that I had promised to reveal to her on the following day.

After the wedding a large party gathered at my father's, but it was agreed that Elizabeth and I should begin our journey by water, sleeping that night at Evian and continuing our voyage on the following day. The day was fair, the wind was with us; everything smiled on our wedding voyage.

Those were the last moments of my life during which I enjoyed a feeling of happiness. We passed rapidly along. I took the hand of Elizabeth.

"You are sorrowful, my love," I said. "Ah! If you knew what I have suffered and what I may yet suffer, you would try to let us enjoy the freedom from sadness that this one day at least permits us to have."

"Be happy, dear Victor," replied Elizabeth. "There is, I hope, nothing to worry you; and be assured that if I do not seem joyous, my heart is contented. What a divine day it is! How happy and peaceful all nature appears!"

The wind, which had up to now carried us along with swiftness, sank at sunset to a light breeze; the soft air just ruffled the water and caused a pleasant motion among the trees as we approached the shore. The sun sank beneath the horizon as we landed, and as I touched the shore, I felt those cares and fears come back to me which soon were to cling to me forever.

It was eight o'clock when we landed; we walked for a short time on the shore and then retired to the inn. The wind, which had fallen in the south, now rose in the west. The moon had reached her summit in the sky and was beginning to go down; the clouds swept across it swifter than the flight of the vulture. Suddenly a heavy rain came down.

I had been calm during the day, but as soon as night came, a thousand fears arose in my mind. I was anxious and watchful; my right hand grasped a pistol hidden in my shirt. Every sound terrified me, but I decided that I would not shrink from the fight until my own life or that of my enemy was over.

Elizabeth asked, "What is it that bothers you, my dear Victor? What is it you fear?"

"Oh! Peace, peace, my love," I replied. "After this night, all will be safe; but this night is dreadful, very dreadful."

I passed an hour in this state of mind. Suddenly I thought about how fearful the fight that I expected would be to my wife, and I asked her to go to bed, resolving not to join her until I had discovered and conquered my enemy.

She left me, and I continued some time walking up and down the passages of the house and inspecting every corner that might be a hiding place. But I discovered no trace of him and was beginning to think that some lucky chance had kept him away, when suddenly I heard a shrill and dreadful scream. It came from the bedroom. As I heard it, the whole truth rushed into my mind. I rushed into the room.

Great God! Why did I not then die! Why am I here to tell the story of the destruction of the purest creature on earth? She was there, lifeless, thrown across the bed, her head hanging down and her pale features covered by her hair. Could I see this and live? Alas!

While I still hung over her, I happened to look up. With a feeling of horror, I saw at the open window that most hideous and hated creature. A grin was on the face of the monster; he seemed to jeer, as with his fiendish finger he pointed toward the corpse of my wife. I rushed toward the window and, drawing the pistol from my shirt, I fired; but he escaped and, running with the swiftness of lightning, he plunged into the lake.

The firing of my pistol brought a crowd into the room. I pointed to the spot where he had disappeared,

I rushed toward the window and fired the pistol.

and we followed the track with boats. After passing several hours, we returned hopeless, most of my companions believing it to have been my imagination about there being a monster.

I was bewildered, in a cloud of wonder and horror. The death of William, the murder of Clerval, and lastly of my wife; even at that moment I did not know if my only remaining friends were safe from the evil of that fiend; my father even now might be writhing under his grasp, and Ernest might be dead at his feet. I started up and resolved to return to Geneva with all possible speed.

Nothing is so painful to the human mind as a great and sudden change. The sun might shine or the clouds might go down: but nothing could appear to me as it had done the day before. A fiend had snatched from me every hope of future happiness; no creature had ever been so miserable as I was. One by one my friends were taken away. I was left alone. I must now tell, in a few words, what remains of my hideous story.

10. Frankenstein Pursues the Monster

I ARRIVED AT Geneva. My father and Ernest yet lived, but the old man had lost the charm and delight of his later years—his Elizabeth. He was unable to rise from his bed, and in a few days he died in my arms.

I was possessed by a maddening rage when I thought of the monster I had created, the miserable demon I had sent abroad into the world for my destruction. I prayed that I might have him within my grasp to bring revenge on his cursed head.

Uncertain how to track the fiend, I wandered for many hours. As night approached, I found myself at the entrance of the cemetery where William, Elizabeth, and my father were buried. I entered it and went to the tomb that marked their graves. Everything was silent except the leaves of the trees, which were shaking in the wind. The night was dark. I knelt on the grass and kissed the earth and cried out, "I swear to chase down the demon who caused this misery, until he or I shall die in mortal combat."

Through the stillness of night, I was answered by a loud and fiendish laugh. A well-known and hated voice whispered, "I am satisfied, miserable wretch! You have determined to live and suffer, and I am satisfied."

I darted toward the spot from which the voice came, but the devil escaped me. Suddenly the moon arose and shone full upon his ghastly body as he fled.

I went after him; and for many months this has been my task. Guided by a slight clue, I followed the windings of the Rhone. On the Mediterranean we both boarded a vessel bound for the Black Sea, but somehow he escaped me. Amidst the wilds of Tartary and Russia, although he still kept out of my reach, I constantly followed in his track. Sometimes the peasants, scared by this horrid monster, informed me of his path; sometimes he himself, who feared that I might despair and die if I lost all trace of him, left some mark to guide me. When the snows came down, I saw and followed the print of his huge step on the white plain.

When I could, I followed the courses of the rivers; but the demon generally avoided these, as it was here that the population collected.

What his feelings were I cannot know. Sometimes, indeed, he left marks in writing on the bark of trees or cut in stone that guided me and brought out my fury. "My power over you is not yet over," he wrote. "Follow me; I seek the everlasting ice of the north, where you will feel the misery of cold and frost, to which I am unfeeling. You will find near where you are a dead rabbit; eat it and gain your strength. You will need it. Come after me; we have yet to fight for our lives, but many hard and miserable hours must you suffer until that period shall arrive."

As I continued my journey northward, the snows thickened and the rivers were covered with ice. Another message he left was in these words: "Prepare for the worst! Wrap yourself in furs and provide yourself with food, for we shall soon enter upon a journey where your sufferings will satisfy my hatred."

Some weeks before this period I had obtained a sledge and dogs and thus traveled across the snows with speed. I was able to gain on him, so much so that when I first saw the ocean he was but one day's journey ahead of me, and I hoped to cut him off before he should reach the shore. I pressed on, and in two days arrived at a wretched seaside village. I asked the natives about the fiend, and they told me a gigantic monster had arrived the night before, armed with a gun and many pistols. He had carried off their store of winter food and, placing it in a sledge, he had stolen their dogs to draw it and had gone on his way.

He had escaped me, and I now faced an almost endless journey across the ice plains and mountainous icebergs, amidst cold that few of the natives could long endure, and which I could not hope to survive. I exchanged my land sledge for one made for the ice-covered ocean, bought a stock of food, and departed from land. I cannot guess how many days have passed since then. Huge and rugged mountains of ice often barred my passage, and I often heard the thunder of the sea beneath. But again the frost came and made the paths of the sea safe.

Once, after the poor dogs that pulled the sledge had climbed to the top of a sloping iceberg, I looked out and suddenly my eye caught a dark speck on the plain of ice ahead. I strained my sight to find out what it could be and uttered a wild cry of excitement when I made out a sledge and the hulking shape of the fiend.

I gave my dogs a good portion of food and then continued my route. The sledge was still visible, and I never again lost sight of it. I gained on it, and after nearly two days' journey, I beheld my enemy at no more than a mile away, my heart bounding within me.

But now, when I appeared almost within grasp of my foe, I lost all trace of him. A ground sea was heard; it thundered as the waters rolled and swelled beneath me. I drove on, but in vain. The wind arose; the sea

The sea had surrounded the piece of ice I was left upon.

roared; and with the shock of an earthquake, it split and cracked open the ice in front of me. In a few minutes the sea had surrounded the piece of ice I was left upon.

Many hours passed; then I saw your ship. I had no idea that ships ever came so far north and was astounded by the sight. I quickly destroyed part of my sledge to construct oars, and with great effort I was able to enter the sea and row my ice raft in the direction of your ship.

Oh, Walton, my friend, must I die and the monster yet live? If I do, swear to me that he shall not escape, that you will seek him out and kill him. Once his words had power over my heart; but do not trust him, and plunge your sword straight into his heart.

11. Walton and the Monster

August 26, 17—

Dearest sister,

You have read this strange and amazing story; and is it not horrifying? Sometimes, in painful agony, he could not continue his tale; at other times, his broken voice could barely utter the words. His tale is told with an appearance of truth, yet I must say that the letters of Felix and Safie, which he showed me, and our sighting of the monster from the ship, brought to me a stronger belief in the truth of his story than his claims to it. Such a monster, then, really exists! Sometimes I tried to gain from Frankenstein the details of how he created the monster, but on this point he refused to tell me anything.

"Are you mad, my friend?" he asked. "Would you create for yourself and the world a demonical enemy? Peace, peace! Learn from my miseries."

Thus a week passed away, while I listened to the strangest tale ever told. Shortly afterward our ship was surrounded by icebergs that allowed of no escape and threatened at every moment to crush us. Finally the ice began to move, and we heard roarings like thunder as the ice cracked in every direction.

My unfortunate guest, meanwhile, was so ill he was confined to his bed.

When the ice cracked behind us and allowed us a passage toward the south, I made the decision to bring my men and the ship back to England.

"Do you, then, really return to England?" asked Victor Frankenstein from his bed.

"Alas!" I told him. "Yes, I cannot lead them further into danger."

"Do so, if you will; but I will not. I must pursue the fiend to the end of my life." Saying this, he tried to spring from the bed, but instead he fell back and fainted.

It was hours before he recovered, and when he did, he called me to come near. "My strength is gone," he said. "I feel that I shall soon die, and that he, my enemy, will live. During these last few days I have been thinking about my life. In a fit of madness, I created a creature and was bound to try to give him happiness. This was my duty; but there was another duty higher than that. That was my duty to my fellow human beings. I was right to refuse to create a mate for the monster. He was wicked; he destroyed my loved ones. I do not even now know where his thirst for vengeance may end. The task of his destruction was mine, but I have failed. Now that you are returning to England, you will have little chance of meeting with him. Farewell, Walton!" He sank into silence. About half an hour later he tried to speak but was unable; he pressed my hand, and his eyes closed forever.

Margaret, what comment can I make on the death of this extraordinary man?

Wait! I hear something. It is midnight; the breeze is blowing. There is a sound of a human voice; it comes from the room where Frankenstein lies dead. I must get up and go look. Good night, my sister.

Reaching out one huge hand, the creature hung over the coffin.

Great God! What a scene has just taken place! I hardly know whether I shall be able to write it down! Yet the tale which I have set down would not be complete without this final event.

I entered the room where Frankenstein lay. Over him hung a creature which I cannot find words to describe—gigantic, monstrous, ugly. As he hung over the coffin, his face was hidden by long locks of ragged hair; but one huge hand, in color and texture like that of a mummy, was reaching out. When he heard the sound of my approach, he sprang toward the window. Never did I see so disgusting and ugly a face. I shut my eyes and called on him to remain.

He paused, looking on me with wonder, and turned toward the lifeless form of his creator.

"In his murder my crimes are done with," he said. "Oh, Frankenstein! What does it matter that I now ask you to pardon me? I destroyed you by destroying all you loved. Alas, he is dead, he cannot answer me."

I approached this giant; I dared not again raise my eyes to his face, there was something so hideous and unearthly in it. "Your sorrow," I said, "is worthless. If you had listened to your conscience, Frankenstein would yet have lived."

"Do you think that I did not then feel agony and sadness? He," the monster continued, pointing to his creator, "he did not suffer in his death one thousandth of the anguish that was mine. Do you think that the groans of Clerval were music to my ears? My heart was made to be awakened by love and kindness, and it was broken by misery and became violent and full of hatred.

"After the murder of Clerval, I returned to Switzerland. I hated myself. But when I found out that he, my creator, dared to hope for happiness from which I was forever barred, then I was filled with a thirst for vengeance. I remembered the threat I had made and decided that I would carry it out. Yet when she died—then I was not miserable. I had cast off all feeling. Evil from then on became my good. The completion of my demonical plan became my passion. And now it is ended; there is my last victim!"

"Wretch!" I said. "You throw a torch into a building, and when it burns up, you sit among the ruins and cry over its destruction. Hypocritical fiend! It is not pity for him that you feel; you are sorry only because the victim is no longer in your power."

"Oh, it is not so—not so," interrupted the creature. "I am content to suffer alone. Once my imagination had dreams of goodness, of fame, of enjoyment. Once I dreamed of meeting with beings who, pardoning my outward form, would love me for the excellent qualities I was capable of showing. I cannot believe that I am the same creature whose thoughts were once filled with beauty and goodness. But it is so; the fallen angel becomes a devil. Yet even Satan had friends and companions; I am alone.

"You, who call Frankenstein your friend, seem to have a knowledge of my crimes and his misfortunes. But in the details he gave you of them he could not sum up the hours and months of misery I suffered. For while I destroyed his hopes, I did not satisfy my own desires. I wanted love and fellowship, and I was rejected. Yes, it is true that I am a wretch. I have murdered the lovely and the helpless; I have strangled the innocent as they slept and grasped to death the throat of those who never injured me or any other living thing. I have brought my creator to misery. There he lies in death. You hate me, but your hatred cannot equal that with which I regard myself.

"I shall leave your ship on the ice raft that brought

me here and shall seek the northernmost point of the world; I shall gather material for my funeral fire and burn this miserable body to ashes. Stained by crimes and torn by sadness, where can I find rest but in death? Farewell! I leave you, the last human these eyes will ever see."

He turned to the figure on the bed and exclaimed, "Farewell, Frankenstein! Destroyed as you were, my agony was still worse than yours. But soon I shall die, and what I now feel will be no longer felt. I shall climb atop my funeral pyre of torturing flames. My ashes will be swept into the sea by the winds. My spirit will sleep in peace. Farewell."

He sprang from the cabin window as he said this, upon the ice raft that lay close to the ship. He was soon carried away by the waves and was lost in darkness and distance.